KING SHIT

STORY BY BRIAN ALAN ELLIS

ILLUSTRATIONS BY WAYLON THORNTON

Shit About the Book

"[*King Shit*] says a lot about class and culture in America. It is a finely wrought gobbet of sputum lobbed at the American middle class proprieties."

Chicago Center for Literature and Photography

"[*King Shit* is] wildly fun and real."

SHELDON LEE COMPTON, author of *Brown Bottle*

"[*King Shit*] is packed with hilarity and a strange sadness that comes from the way it reflects our own debauched nights."

Verbicide

"[*King Shit*] took me back—into a drunken heap of trouble every week. [Its characters are] enjoyable weirdos all functioning as part of the same dysfunctional world..."

Razorcake

"[*King Shit*] is a night-long journey of drugs and violence going nowhere fast, albeit as humorously as possible..."

BEN TANZER, author of *Sex and Death*

"[*King Shit* is] an amusing journey through a single evening of tomfoolery and disappointment."

NATHANIEL TOWER, author of *Use, Remove, Repeat*

"[*King Shit*'s] mix of prose and occasional illustration reminded me just a bit of some of the Bukowski/Crumb collaborations—quite a gritty romp."

DAVID S. ATKINSON, author of *Not Quite So Stories*

"Ellis's uncanny ability to humbly dress characters in yesterday's dirty, beer-soaked, rumpled clothing and march them back and forth from place to place like it ain't no big thang speaks directly to the insecurities in each of us."

The Next Best Book Blog

"[*King Shit* is a] nihilistic romp, a misanthropic tangent—a 'fuck you.' Why? Because fuck you."

RYAN WERNER, author of *Soft*

Other Shit by the Author

*A Series of Pained Facial Expressions Made
While Shredding Air Guitar*

Sexy Time in the Spook House, Oh Yeah!

Something Good, Something Bad, Something Dirty

*The Mustache He's Always Wanted but
Could Never Grow*

33 Fragments of Sick-Sad Living

KING SHIT

An Illustrated Novella by
BRIAN ALAN ELLIS and
WAYLON THORNTON

HOUSE OF VLAD PRODUCTIONS
Super Fun Land • USA

A HOUSE OF VLAD PRODUCTION
© 2016, © 2014 by Brian Alan Ellis and Waylon Thornton

Third Paperback Edition: July, 2016

All rights reserved. No part of this book may be used or reproduced in any manner whatsoever without written permission from the publisher, with the exception of excerpts used for critical essays and reviews.

This is a work of fiction. Any resemblance to real persons, living or dead, is purely coincidental.

A version of *King Shit* previously appeared at *Curbside Quotidian*, summer 2011; an excerpt from *King Shit* previously appeared at *CLASH*, spring 2014.

"Funny, Doomed, Water-Damaged, Drunk, High, and Unfiltered"
© 2014 by Bud Smith

Book design: Percy Hearst
Illustrations: Waylon Thornton
Author photograph: Christia Nunnery
Illustrator photograph courtesy of Waylon Thornton

brianalanellis.tumblr.com / @brianalanellis

waylonthornton.tumblr.com / @waylonthornton

houseofvlad.tumblr.com / @HouseofVlad

ISBN-10: 0692220186
ISBN-13: 978-0692220184

FUNNY, DOOMED, WATER-DAMAGED, DRUNK, HIGH, AND UNFILTERED: An Introduction

"That's right. I'm the king, baby! Da'other King!"

Elvis McAllister

I GREW UP IN FLEA MARKETS. I grew up in a campground in New Jersey. I grew up at the Seaside Boardwalk, a slimy place where everything was half tilted and bizarre. *King Shit* reminds me of where I come from. *King Shit* reminds me of the kind of art I used to seek out when I was browsing through Captain Video, looking at VHS in cardboard sleeves. Brian Alan Ellis is writing works that are all these things: funny, doomed, water-damaged, drunk, high, and unfiltered. I like that. I identify with that. Maybe his characters are saying some things that shouldn't be said in public, and hooray for them. This is a work of fiction written outside of a writer's workshop, but instead, maybe written in the basement of a VFW hall, right before the hardcore bands show up. Right before the spiked punks in their leather jackets show up. Right before the night gets weird, violent, skewed. The other good thing about this book, is that it's illustrated in a way that is reminiscent of one of my favorite books, Vonnegut's *Breakfast of Champions*. The drawings in both books are perfect and they give absolutely zero fucks whatsoever. *King Shit* is a bar crawl adventure, written as a novella. Can be read on the toilet, but your ass will be numb by the time you're finished. Can be read at the DMV waiting to get called, but you'll probably start flipping chairs and screaming when the book is done and they still haven't called you. Can be read at a bar. But that's kind of silly. Bars are for other things. I recommend reading this one in jail or at work, can't go wrong there. When a book takes itself this un-seriously, I can't stop doing the happy-happy dance.

BUD SMITH, 2014

ONE

ELVIS McALLISTER SAID, "How 'bout them drinks?" Then he lit cigarettes for both him and his buddy Ralph. "It's been a rough one."

Nearby, a fat Mexican wearing thigh-high leather boots struggled down Sixth Avenue. No one could tell whether the man was drunk, clumsy, or just not accustomed to the footwear chosen this particular evening.

"Did yuh invite me out tonight 'cause I'm yuh friend?" asked Ralph. "Or was it 'cause yuh knew I'd probably be the one drivin' us both home?"

"Aw shucks," said Elvis. "You know me better'an that. Yuh my boy."

The Mexican had on a Santa Claus costume—though it was July, not December—and so his whole body jingled—"jingled all the way," many onlookers had remarked—through Seventh Street, then Eighth, stopping between Ninth and Tenth, in front of Elvis and Ralph.

"Can Santa have a smoke, little boys?" asked the Mexican. A plastic green bucket dangled from an arm he had propped inside a sling.

"Sure," said Ralph, placing a couple of long cigarettes inside the bucket.

"Just be careful in them things," said Elvis. "All the kids'll be real sad if yuh fall and get the hurts."

The Mexican said, "Muchas gracias mis amigos," before taking off down Eleventh.

TWO

ELVIS McALLISTER RAN a furniture factory. His job was to oversee orders and to make sure his employees—he called them his "boys"—did whatever they were supposed to. But mainly he would just stand around for hours, drinking coffee and telling stories.

Elvis's stories, true or fabricated, were always a hit with the "boys." During lunch they'd listen and laugh while wolfing down homemade sandwiches, salty potato chips, prepackaged pastries, cigarettes, energy drinks—all of it catching on their uniforms and, if they had them, their beards too.

Elvis's favorite story, the one he took most pride in telling, was the one regarding his name.

The story went that Mrs. McAllister, for various and ever-changing reasons, named her only son after Elvis Presley, a Memphis rock and roll singer known famously as "The King." It was rumored, however, that McAllister's first name was actually inspired by one Elvis Costello, a nebbish Brit-rocker who, compared to the more revered Presley, was practically a cult concern.

Regardless, a first name was the only thing Elvis McAllister would ever share with Mr. Presley: he didn't look like the earlier, thinner Elvis; nor did he resemble the later, heavier Elvis. He was more like an incongruous Elvis, one who had never really existed—scrawny, though pudgy in the abdomen, with hair much too thin to even be combed properly.

But he had charm.

THREE

"**TOMMY!**" **ELVIS CALLED** to the bartender. "A Stardust martini for Liberace's asshole... and f'me, the usual."

"Of course," said Tommy the bartender. "That means the cheapest beer we got on tap, then, right?" He filled a mug up with cheap beer. "Why can't yuh order a tall gin 'n' tonic or two?" He slid the beer towards Elvis. "I got kids to feed, motherfucker."

"Tommy once tol' me," Ralph whispered to Elvis, "that he likes dressin' up in women's clothes."

"Funny guy," said Elvis, slurping foam off his beer. "Funny guy."

Ralph looked over at an old man with several empty glasses lined up in front of him. "Real classy Fred Blassie we got here," he said to Elvis.

The old man began slurring to himself—or to someone only he could see. "Not much to live for these days," he said. "Everything's an empty fix—monotony, any whichaway you slice it. They say that just being alive should be enough to go on, but no, goddamn it! Everyone and everything outside of you just being alive will... will... It'll make damned sure that it isn't..."

The last few lines of the old man's monologue proved a courageous struggle as his head fell forward and slammed against the bar.

"Get 'im another, will yuh?" Elvis said to Tommy. "On me!"

"You couldn't afford it, you cheap pussy," said Tommy.

FOUR

A MAN IN A MUSKY, lavender-colored suit (polyester) patted Elvis's shoulder.

He turned.

"Hey, buddy," said the man in the suit, exhuming a moist laugh, "I remember you." He dabbed his lips with a napkin. "You was with those big-tittied girls that one night." He brought his face up close to Elvis's ear. "They said you gots a BIG PURPLE DICK!"

Elvis pounded the man in the suit's fist and said, "Hellz yeah. That was some wild-ass shit, huh?" Truth was he hadn't a clue as to who those "big-tittied" girls were, and this saddened him.

"Yuh damn right it was!" The man in the suit chuckled. "I tell yuh, those bitches—"

The man in the suit's head quickly turned, as did other heads, once the fat Mexican dressed as Santa swaggered into the bar. This time, instead of the plastic green bucket, he had a rainbow-colored Chihuahua tucked snuggly inside the curve of his sling.

"Hey, Chiquita!" said the man in the suit. "Where you goin'? You remember that night..."

Elvis and Ralph moved down a few seats as the man in the suit went after the Mexican with the dog.

"That fella in the suit was kinda cute," said Ralph.

"Quit foolin'," said Elvis.

"He was."

"Bleck!"

"Aw, what's wrong, McAllister? Jealous?"

"Fuck off!" Elvis stood. "I gotta piss."

"Shake it for me, King," Ralph kidded.

"That's right. I'm the king, baby! Da'other King!" Elvis shouted this from halfway across the bar.

Nobody cared.

FIVE

ELVIS WALKED THROUGH the door with the word MEN on it, and squinted, adjusting his eyes to the blue fluorescent lights flickering on and off.

Like stepping in a *Twilight Zone* turd, he thought.

Then he noticed, in the cracked mirror above the urinal, two men, rockabilly-greaser types, sharing a bathroom stall; the door to the stall was missing, so Elvis could see in real good.

Probably poofs, he thought.

Then he noticed that one of them looked sick: legs giving out, heavy sweats, spittle, eyes rolling back into his skull, pompadour sadly wilting.

Probably addicts, he thought again.

The sickly looking rockabilly then crumpled over and began vomiting into the urinal beside Elvis.

Elvis shuffled over some and tried pissing in the sink. "If you need me, I'll be over here," he said.

"He's straight," said the not-so-sickly-looking rockabilly, dragging the puke-sick one through the bathroom door and out into the bar.

With the greasers gone, Elvis could finally urinate in peace—"Like a real man oughta," he'd say. Then he wondered what it would be like to piss on a female. Some of the men at his job said they had, but Elvis didn't believe them.

He flushed.

SIX

ELVIS, WHILE SHUFFLING THROUGH the crowd to retrieve his seat, saw Ralph talking with an attractive brunette. He thought the brunette—she wore a snug pink and black outfit, with heels and garter stockings—resembled a small, voluptuous (though bow legged) burlesque dancer he'd known from years back. "Well, if isn't Miss Debra Swank!" he called out to her.

The attractive brunette turned, and seeing Elvis her eyes lit up. "In the flesh," she cooed.

"And what wonderful, snowy white flesh it is," said Elvis. "If I could snort yuh up my nose right now, I would." He took Debra into his arms and twirled her round. "Ah, my incandescent flower," he said, looking her over. "Still got that cute upturned nose, workin' that sass! Yuh still boss, baby—*real boss*." Then he turned to Ralph and said, "Not much use for them parts Debz been showin' yuh, huh? Youz a cocksmith!"

Elvis then pinched Debra's ass. She squirmed and said, "Your friend Ralph, here, is so polite. What happened to your manners, mister?"

"Life got hold of me. Shook me round a bit." Elvis lit a cigarette. "This is what settled, baby."

SEVEN

"SO WHAT'S IT YUH DO, DEBRA?" asked Ralph—all Gentlemen Jim about it, Elvis thought.

"I used to star in my own burlesque show," she said proudly. "But now I go to beauty school."

"Beauty school?" Elvis dribbled beer down the front of his shirt. "Pshaw! What d'yuh need flippin' beauty school for? Hell, yuh already a natural—a natural *beauty*, that is."

Debra blushed and said, "Don't be fresh!"

"So," said Elvis, "who yuh livin' wit' now?" He was curious as to whether or not Debra had roommates, or—worse, he felt—a live-in boyfriend.

"My boyfriend," she said.

"Is that so?" said Elvis. "What's yuh boy-toy do? Bet he ain't much. Bet I could take 'im."

"He's a bouncer," said Debra.

Elvis looked away. He didn't want that kind of trouble.

EIGHT

"HEY, I WANNA DANCE!" Debra shouted as she shot up out of Elvis's arms—like a bullet with titties, he thought—and then climbed on top of a pool table.

Elvis went over to the jukebox. He took a smashed dollar bill from his pocket, flattened it against the edge of a table, and then paid the machine. "King of the Night Time World," the second song off of KISS *Destroyer* (one of Debra's favorites, he'd remembered), started playing:

> *I'm the king of the night time world*
> *And you're my headlight queen*
> *I'm the king of the night time world*
> *Come live your secret dream*

Elvis turned to Ralph. "Looks real good, don't she?" he said. Ralph agreed, commenting on how impressive it was that Debra's small body could move the way it did—"with her being bull legged and all," he added.

"Watch this," said Elvis, knowing that Debra was about to pull her top off and begin swinging it above her head. "The big finale."

Off came the top.

"Wow," said Ralph, "she ain't even wearin' no bra!"

It was true: Debra was braless, though her nipples were covered with pieces of electrical tape. Either way, the men (gay and straight) all loved it—as did several lesbians; they whistled and clapped and grabbed themselves, whereas the majority of heterosexual women found Debra's performance to be quite obnoxious.

Then things got out of hand: dollar bills flew; furniture, bottles and people were knocked over; and many of the liquored-up patrons started to fondle Debra.

"Don't look so good," said Ralph. "You should probably do somethin'."

"Yuh right," said Elvis. "I'll play hero. And after I save 'er, she'll have no choice but to leave wit' me. It's brilliant."

But it was too late.

NINE

THROUGH BODIES, BILLS, and furniture—tossing people twice his size out of his way and into the air—a stocky, bald-headed dwarf picked Debra up with one hand—kicking and screaming as she was—and hoisted her up over his shoulder.

"Time ta go home, Debra," ordered the tiny voice.

And no one stopped him. They knew better.

"That must be the boyfriend," said Ralph, casually sipping his glittering martini.

"Some bouncer, this," said Elvis.

"Now's yuh chance, Romeo," said Ralph. "Go saves yuh Rapunzel."

"Fuck that!" said Elvis. "Just look at the guy. Built like a goddamn professional wrestler—and only like two and a half, maybe three and a half feet of 'im!"

"I've seen yuh lose many women, McAllister. But never like that."

"Very funny."
"He was kinda cute," said Ralph.
"Fuck off!"
Elvis tottered away as though he'd been shot.
"Hey, McAllister! Where yuh goin'?"
"Fresh air," he wheezed, shouldering through all the commotion.

TEN

ELVIS, ONCE RALPH HAD found him, was sitting on a curb. His head was in his hands, and he was mumbling to himself about the dwarf—"that pint-sized brawler, that little bastard from Hades"—who had ruined his chances with Debra.

Ralph said, "We live in a sick one, King," and he took Elvis's arm and pulled him up from the curb. And as they started for the car, the man in the suit rode by on a bicycle with Hendrix ("Purple Haze") blaring out of a small radio fastened to the handlebars—clutching him from behind was the fat Mexican; his rainbow Chihuahua sat perched—"like gay E.T.," Ralph noted—in the front basket, just above the small radio.

"Hey, BIG PURPLE!" the man in the suit hollered. "I dedicate this song to you, BROTHA!"

The Mexican then shouted something in Spanish to the man in the suit, and their rickety vehicle bounced into oncoming traffic.

Elvis and Ralph cheered them on, knowing that the trio would make it safely to whichever destination they'd set their hearts on, no matter what.

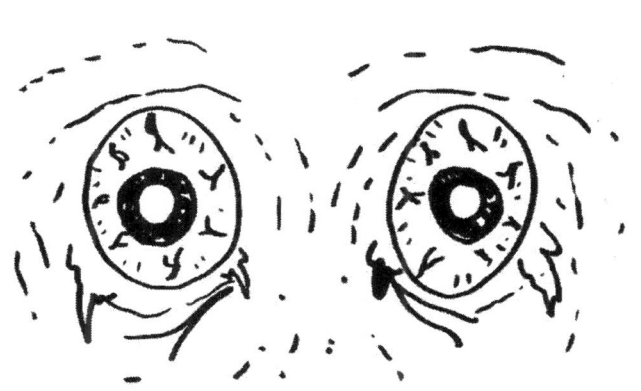

ELEVEN

PASSING THIRD, RALPH POINTED to something on First. "Hey," he said, "ain't that your ex over there?"

The woman he thought was Elvis's ex stood beneath a street lamp. She was cussing at someone.

"That's Donna all right," said Elvis. "What the hell's she doin' to that poor sumbitch?"

Donna was swinging her purse at the man Elvis deemed a "poor sumbitch."

"I'm glad she's finally seein' other people," said Ralph.

"Talk to me, yuh FUCKING COCKSUCKER!" Donna howled as the boyfriend staggered drunkenly. She railed him again with her purse, and he almost toppled over entirely but was somehow able to balance himself. Steadied, he took a swig of beer. When Donna pulled back to hit him once more, he spit a mouthful into her face.

"Did yuh see that, Ralph?"

"I'm afraid so, King."

"That," said Elvis, "was the funniest damn thing I ever did see!"

Donna, soaked, her makeup streaked across her face, looked over and saw Elvis laughing and pointing at her. Before getting into her car and leaving, she yelled many expletives at him.

"I think I'm gonna go up and congratulate the guy," said Elvis.

"Don't do it," warned Ralph. "He looks piiiiissed."

Elvis didn't listen. He went up to the guy, hand outstretched, and said, "Nice job, buddy, I really like—"

With a quick left, the guy sent Elvis sailing towards concrete. Ralph then pulled out a stiletto blade and began waving it in front of the guy's face—"like it was some limp cock," the guy would later tell Donna, once they had reconciled.

"A tough queer, that Ralph," is what Elvis would have said—had he of course not been unconscious.

TWELVE

THERE WAS A GROWING EMPTINESS inside Elvis as he and Ralph continued towards the car. (Emptiness was not the only thing growing for Elvis; his eye had swollen to an impressive proportion, courtesy of the punch he had just taken.)

"Lemme get a cigarette," said Elvis.

"Yuh always say my cigs are fairy," said Ralph.

"Yeah, well, I'm desperate," said Elvis. "I ran outta mine."

Ralph lit Elvis's cigarette for him. "Did yuh enjoy yuhself tonight?"

"Are yuh kiddin'?" said Elvis. "Tonight was murder!"

"Aw, come on," said Ralph. "It wasn't that bad."

Elvis thought about it. "All right, all right," he said. "I guess it wasn't a bad night. Some funny stuff happened, yeah. It was a *good* night, all right—just not a *great* night."

"So what woulda made it a great night, King?"

"Had I got laid," said Elvis. "Then it woulda been a great night."

"The night's still young," said Ralph.

"No," said Elvis. "The night is dead... and gettin' deader by the minute." He took a deep, suffocating drag from his cigarette. "Seriously," he said, "there ain't no chance in hell of me gettin' laid at this hour... unless I fucked you. But yuh ain't my type, Ralph."

"Hey, I wonder," said Ralph, "what the boys'll say when they finds out a homo saved yuh life."

"Do me a favor, Ralph, and don't tell nobody. Okay?"

"All right," he said. "But can I tell 'em 'bout Mr. Big Purple? Or cholo Saint Nick?"

"YOLO Claus? Hell no," said Elvis, "I'm usin' those."

"What yuh think happened to 'em, anyways?"

"Our midget probably happened to 'em," said Elvis, tossing away his cigarette.

"I think he was a dwarf," said Ralph.

Elvis said, "The hell difference does it make? He still fucked up my chances."

THIRTEEN

ELVIS AND RALPH FOUND the car. They got in. Ralph started it up; Elvis messed with the radio.

"Oh," said Ralph, "guess what Tommy called you, when you left to take a piss?"

"What'd Tommy call me when I went to take a piss?"

"He called you King Shit." Ralph laughed

"King Shit, huh? Well, at least he got the first part right."

"Yeah," said Ralph, "and at least a homo saved yuh life."

Elvis didn't say anything for a while. Then "Heartbreak Hotel" came on.

"That's what I'm talkin' 'bout," said Elvis, turning it up. "Floyd Cramer. Scotty Moore. Chet Atkins. D.J. Fontana. Bill Black. All his boys."

"All fags," said Ralph.

Elvis, letting the music radiate through him in waves, sat in silence. He had a dumb, serene look on his face. He wasn't bothered that Ralph had referred to Presley's backing band as homosexuals. After all, like Mr. Presley, he was still "The King," and somehow the days and nights went down easier and were a little brighter for him this way.

Come Monday he'd really shine.

Shit About the Author

BRIAN ALAN ELLIS edits the literary journal *Tables Without Chairs*, and is the author of several books. He lives in Tallahassee, Florida, and is an official card-carrying member of the KISS Army.

Shit About the Illustrator

WAYLON THORNTON is a guitar man and artist, native to the North Florida town of Lake Butler, where he lives with his wife, Meg, and son, Dex Wray. He is a firm believer in the power of the American cheeseburger, a cold Cherry Coke, and cheap guitars.

HOUSE OF VLAD

Made in the USA
Middletown, DE
20 December 2018